P9-AOD-180

JAMES PRELLER

NIGHTMARELAND

SCARY TALES

Illustrated by IACOPO BRUNO

FEIWEL AND FRIENDS
New York

A FEIWEL AND FRIENDS BOOK
An Imprint of Macmillan

NIGHTMARELAND. Text copyright © 2014 by James Preller. Illustrations
copyright © 2014 by Iacopo Bruno. All rights reserved. Printed in
the United States of America by R. R. Donnelley & Sons Company,
Harrisonburg, Virginia. For information, address Feiwel and Friends,
175 Fifth Avenue, New York, N.Y. 10010.

Feiwel and Friends books may be purchased for business or promotional
use. For information on bulk purchases, please contact the Macmillan
Corporate and Premium Sales Department at (800) 221-7945 x5442 or by
e-mail at specialmarkets@macmillan.com.

Library of Congress Cataloging-in-Publication Data Available

ISBN: 978-1-250-01892-2 (hardcover) / 978-1-250-01893-9 (paperback)
978-1-250-06193-5 (ebook)

Book design by Ashley Halsey

Feiwel and Friends logo designed by Filomena Tuosto

First Edition: 2014

10 9 8 7 6 5 4 3 2 1

mackids.com

This book is for Bill Prosser and Karen Terlecky of "Literate Lives," early friends in cyberspace and now in real life, which is even better.

START

CONTENTS

IT'S NOT REAL.

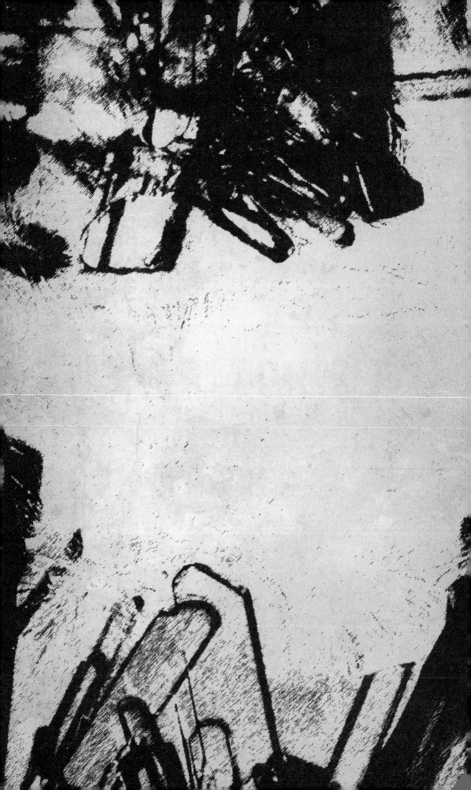

AARON WHEELER JUST GOT A STRANGE, NEW VIDEO GAME CALLED NIGHTMARELAND. IT SUCKS AARON RIGHT IN.

BUT THAT'S NOT UNUSUAL. AARON COULD PLAY VIDEO GAMES ALL DAY. THE REAL WORLD JUST FADES AWAY.

THIS TIME, AARON IS WHISKED AWAY TO AN EMPTY GRAVEYARD. HE FINDS HIMSELF ALL ALONE, CAUGHT IN A SNOWSTORM. A HOWL COMES FROM THE NEARBY WOODS.

HOOOOOWL!

IT IS THE CRY OF WOLVES.
AND THERE IS NO WAY OUT.

ENTER AT YOUR OWN RISK

Aaron flipped through the bargain rack in the back of the video store. He paused to read the title on a video game case: **NIGHTMARELAND**.

He picked it up. The lettering looked fierce, but it was the cover picture that captured Aaron's attention—two sinister, bloodshot eyes peered out from under a bed. No matter how he held the video game, the eyes followed Aaron. He moved the case from side to side, up and down. Still, the eyes stared directly at him. Almost . . . directly *into* him.

Pretty creepy, Aaron thought. But then again, he liked creepy stuff.

Everything in the cover illustration was dark, except for a splash of bright red blood on the floor.

Aaron glanced around. A few scruffy guys in saggy pants wandered around the store. Hardcore gamers, obviously. They looked older than Aaron, who was nearly ten. Two other teenaged boys stood by a rack of comic books, leafing through the pages, cracking jokes. Aaron missed his sister, Addy, who chose to wait in the car—music blaring, no doubt. She had told him, "Ten minutes, Aaron. That's it."

He'd already been in there for fifteen.

Aaron flipped over the game case.

Five words ran across the top like yellow tape at a crime scene:

ENTER AT YOUR OWN RISK!

He read the game description.

"Be warned: **NIGHTMARELAND** is more than a game. *Much* more. It is the wind in the graveyard, it is the whisper in the keyhole, the claw across the windowpane. It is the knife, the fang, and the razor. It is the deep, dark corners of your own imagination— where your secret fears become real. Where you become the hunted one."

Okaaaaay, Aaron thought. He dropped the case back into the bin. It was on sale and cheap, only $10.95. Which was good, because that was about all he had in his jeans pocket, gift money from old, sweet Grams, who still thought a pair of Abraham Lincolns could buy something in this world.

Aaron had never heard of the game, and he knew all of the popular ones. His friends in school talked video games nonstop, and everybody bought the same ones. If **NIGHTMARELAND** was any good, Aaron should have heard about it. But maybe for that very reason, Aaron reached out and picked up the box again. He was definitely curious. *It might be the only copy in the universe*, he told himself. *Or at least, the only one in Dublin, Ohio.*

A black-haired girl with dark eye makeup sat at the counter. She hunched forward with her feet tucked under her chair, reading from an old paperback called *The Sirens of Titan*.

"Is this game any good?" Aaron asked. "I never heard of it."

The girl wore clunky bracelets and silver

rings on most of her fingers. She glanced at Aaron and shrugged. "Sorry, I just work here. Those games are all the same to me."

He turned at the sound of his sister's voice. "Aaron, are you coming or what?"

Addy stood at the entrance door, trying to look angry. It didn't fit her. She was too nice.

"I'm almost done." Aaron uncrumpled twelve dollars and handed them to the cashier.

"Oh. Hi, Addy!" one of the skinny, high school-aged guys called to his sister. He had freckles and red, corkscrew hair. "Are you here to get the new DEMONS OF DARKNESS video game? It was just released today and—"

"No, Freddy, I'm here to pick up my little brother," she said. "I don't play video games."

"Too bad, man," Freddy snorted. "You're missing out on some cool times."

Addy didn't reply. She didn't want to hurt poor Freddy's feelings.

Aaron received his change and headed out the door.

"Hey, yo, Addy's little bro," Freddy called. "Whatcha get?"

Aaron held up the box.

Freddy shook his thick, curly mane and said, "Never heard of it, kid. Guess it stinks to be you."

THE HOODED FIGURE

Aaron climbed into the passenger seat. It felt strange to drive with Addy, who had finally gotten her license after failing her first driving test. Talk about scary. Aaron made sure to buckle up.

"Mom's at some big conference in Columbus tonight. She won't be back until late," Addy said. "I'm your babysitter."

"I don't need a babysitter," Aaron replied.

"Well, tough. You're nine years old—

someone has to watch over you," Addy countered.

"Does she pay you?"

"Oh, please." Addy tightened her grip on the steering wheel.

"I'm *almost* ten," Aaron said. "I don't need—"

"I know, Aaron," Addy interrupted. "Just chill, okay? You know it's been tough for Mom."

Aaron watched the houses slide past outside the car window. His father had moved out six months ago. Just like that, he was gone. Aaron didn't know exactly what happened. Nobody told him much. But he could see the hurt in his mother's eyes. The way she sometimes drifted through the house like a ghost. He wondered if his mother could keep it together to still pay the bills, or if maybe they'd have to move to a smaller house. Maybe a different town.

Would she be okay?

Would *they* be okay?

Aaron wasn't sure.

"Tell you what," Addy chirped, "I've got to study for a massive economics test. If you aren't a pain, I'll let you stay up extra late."

"Cool," Aaron agreed. "I'll play Xbox. Can we order pizza?"

All in all, it wasn't a bad deal. Aaron had a new video game, no homework, and no one to tell him to limit his screen time. He didn't like turning off the television.

Aaron was the kind of kid who could get lost in a video game. The world faded to gray. Friends, family, even food—nothing else mattered to Aaron when he plugged into a game. These days, with so much unhappiness at home, Aaron spent lots of time lost in video games.

He walked into the TV room. Large bay windows gave a view of their spacious backyard and swimming pool, covered over now with a tarp because of winter. There were no nearby neighbors, just the yard, the woods, and the municipal golf course beyond that, called "Muni" for short. It was only 4:30 and already nearly dusk. Winter in Ohio.

He slid the game disk into the slot and pushed PLAY. The scene opened with a hooded figure standing alone in a snowy field. Something about the hooded figure felt familiar to Aaron—maybe it was the shape of his body.

Aaron pushed the left analog stick and the figure trudged through the shin-deep snow until he came to a large iron gate. It towered at least twelve feet high. Aaron pushed a blue button—the figure's hands grabbed the gate. Strange. Aaron's fingers suddenly felt cold, as if he could imagine exactly what the game character was feeling. He toggled the right analog stick and the gate shook. The muscles in Aaron's arms tightened. He relaxed his fingers, and the figure in the video game allowed his hands to drop.

Usually with a new game it took a few minutes to figure out how the controller worked, which button did what. Every game was a little different. Yet with this one, Aaron didn't have to think. It all came naturally. He pushed buttons and the figure did exactly what Aaron desired. It was as if Aaron simply had to *think* it and the figure responded.

The boy—for some reason, Aaron thought of the figure as a boy, not a man—peered through the gate. Ancient tombstones stood and leaned in uneven rows. It began to snow. Fat white flakes drifted down, slowly covering the hooded figure's head and shoulders.

Aaron took the controller, pushed a few buttons, toggled forward—and the gate opened with a low groan. He stepped forward, shivering, and entered the graveyard.

FANGS GLEAMING IN THE MOONLIGHT

Aaron? I'm talking to you."

Aaron blinked, looked up, and saw Addy beside him. He pulled the headset off his head.

"I'm going upstairs. Do you need anything before I disappear into my textbook?"

He shook his head.

"Are you okay?" Addy asked. "You seem a little out of it."

Aaron kept his eyes fixed on the television

screen. A part of him felt like it was still in that graveyard.

"Maybe you should take a break," Addy suggested. "Go outside, get some fresh air?"

"No, I want to do this."

That was the end of the conversation.

Aaron felt a powerful connection to the figure in the video game as he moved through the desolate graveyard. It was as if Aaron could imagine exactly what it felt like to be in that place.

It was as if . . .

No, it couldn't be.

He was at home. Safe and sound. Sitting in the corner of an L-shaped couch. Snug as a bug. A bowl of cereal at his side. Dry, no milk, no spoon, the way he liked it.

Aaron touched the tip of his nose. It was damp and cold. He glanced at the end of his finger. He watched a solitary snowflake melt away.

HOW COULD THAT BE POSSIBLE?

―〰〰―

With the controller in his hands, Aaron *became* the figure in the snow.

Walking in the graveyard, he shivered. Aaron blew warm air on his cold fingers. It didn't help. His legs felt heavy pushing through the thick snowfall. He continued on toward pale, yellow lights in the far distance. An old castle, perhaps. Not too far. He'd arrive in ten minutes, cold but happy, grateful for a warm fire. Ready for the next test in his adventure.

Tall trees moaned in Aaron's ears. Wind whistled through bare branches. The long limbs swayed like the arms of a great and groaning creature. The snow fell harder now, heavier.

He pulled the thick robe tight around his shoulders. Aaron focused on the lights ahead of him. He'd played enough video games to know that's where he needed to be.

Aaron had to find shelter, fast.

He became aware of movement amidst the trees. A dance of shadows. Black shapes shivered in the silence, loping from dark to dark, obscured by the swirling snow, hidden by tree trunks and shadows. The cold leaked into Aaron's bones. His toes hurt. The dry snow crunched beneath his feet and he walked to that rhythm.

CRUNCH, CRUNCH.
PAUSE.
CRUNCH-CRUNCH.

Aaron knew he was being watched. He felt the pressure of eyes, like icy hands on his back. There was something out there. A threat. He felt vulnerable in the graveyard. Nowhere to run, nowhere to hide. Now the clouds shifted and moonlight shined full upon the frozen ground. Aaron could make out names on the tombstones. *Barrett*, *Shaw*, *Glassman*. It comforted him to read the names. But in the dark woods to Aaron's left and right, everything remained unknown— shades of gray, shadows of black. The trees formed tall, dark, vertical lines. The rest was nothingness, as empty as an abandoned warehouse.

He glimpsed the shadows that moved

soundlessly amidst the trees, melting into the dark.

They loped on four paws.

Like dogs.

Like wolves.

Aaron saw their eyes, silver slivers of light, staring at him, waiting.

He saw small clouds of their hot breath appear and disappear among the trees. *How many wolves were there?* he wondered. He imagined that he could smell the foul stench of their mouths, crushed bones, and rotted flesh. *What did they eat?* he wondered.

When he moved—slowly, cautiously—the eyes of the wolves moved with him. They meant him great harm. He knew it in his bones.

Wolves hunted in packs. Aaron had learned that in school. The media specialist, Mrs. Grabbe, had made him do a project about endangered species. Aaron had picked wolves. Last year, Aaron even dreamed of wolves. Horrible, vivid nightmares. When wolves attacked their prey, the lead wolf often leaped for the neck, clamping down with powerful jaws. The others in the pack would snap at the prey's legs, each tooth like a knife digging into its flesh. Then the pack would pull the hunted animal to the ground, and it was soon over. The wolves would bite into the victim's soft belly. They would howl in triumph, then dip their muzzles to lick warm blood.

Aaron knew that the wolves meant to follow him and then . . . they would attack as a pack from all sides.

He slipped and fell. Aaron quickly rose, steadying himself. He spun around fearfully, hands lifted in defense.

There was nothing there.

Aaron was alone in the clearing of a valley, surrounded by woods.

Just a boy in the snow.

Except he was being hunted by wolves.

mm

It felt so real, so real.

Aaron put down the handset, rubbed his eyes. He grabbed a fistful of dry cereal. The house was silent, his sister upstairs in her room. It was dark outside, night had fallen without his notice. And with it, snowfall. He returned to the video game.

And that's when Aaron first understood that he wasn't playing a game anymore. It was more like . . . the game was playing him. Aaron was inside the world of **NIGHTMARELAND**, inside the fantasy within the television set.

He was no longer sitting on a big, comfy couch. Oh, his body was still there. The shell, the husk. A big sack of water, as Addy, the future scientist, had once explained. But the real Aaron—the person inside the body, the brain and the heart—had traveled somewhere else.

Somewhere outside his body.

Aaron had merged with the figure in the graveyard.

OWWWWWWL, HOWWWWWWWL!

The wolves cried, one after another. Then he heard them, padding through the snow, moving faster, coming at him from out of the darkness.

White teeth gleaming in the pretty moonlight.

FIRE BOY

Aaron had to think fast.

He searched his mind for an answer. Aaron had spent hours each day playing video games. He knew how they worked. He reviewed the situation: He was alone in a graveyard with a pack of wolves. It was a puzzle to solve, that's all.

What he needed now, he thought, was a weapon.

A shield, a club, a—

What's this?

A thick stick poked out of the snow. Aaron grasped it, sniffed. One end smelled of kerosene. Was it a torch?

He felt something in the deep pocket of his cloak. It was a splinter of wood about the length of his pinky. He recognized it as an old-fashioned match. Aaron had seen waterproof matches like this one before— his father always brought them on family camping trips.

Back when they used to be a family, Aaron thought.

Five wolves arrayed themselves behind Aaron in a loose semi-circle. He saw that the wolves were thin and ragged, with ribs showing through. They held their ground, waiting for something. A signal? Or a show of weakness? Aaron knew there must be another wolf—the leader of the pack—

circling beyond his field of vision. That's how the attack would start. A leap from the dark. Claws out, teeth bared.

Aaron struck the match against the dry fabric of his jeans. It sparked. He held the match to the end of the torch and **WHOOSH**, it burst into flame. A flume of black smoke billowed up to the sky. Aaron waved the torch in a fiery circle.

The wolves yipped and backed away, ears dropped down close to their skulls.

Aaron twirled again and saw one old, black wolf, much larger than the others. Its eyes were yellow, its muzzle gone gray. An ugly scar zigzagged across its face. The great beast inched forward, a low growl rumbling in its throat.

"Aaaah!" Aaron shouted. He lunged forward and jabbed the torch at the wolf, nearly striking it on the snout. A spark landed on the beast's coat—*the wolf gave a sudden cry*—and rolled in the snow to kill the flame.

Feeling new courage, Aaron screamed at the other wolves, waving the torch like a madman. The wolves scampered to a safe distance from him, confused and wary. Yet they did not retreat fully into the woods. Hunger kept them close. Empty bellies made them brave.

"That's right, you nasty dogs! I am Aaron—and I have *fire* now!" He looked back over his shoulder. The old castle was near. But between the castle and Aaron stood a barrier: a tall, iron fence. There was no opening to slip through. No gate, even. Aaron did not think he could climb up fast enough before the wolves would jump and snap at his legs. No, that would not work. He turned again. The pack inched closer.

At that instant, Aaron understood that expression "wolfish grin."

They seemed to be smiling.

Long tongues licked hungry lips.

He was trapped.

Then he felt it, the strangest sensation of all: Someone else was watching him, too.

AND THEN ADDY SCREAMED

*D*ing-dong.

The doorbell sounded through the house.

"Aaron? It's the pizza guy. Get the door," Addy called from her upstairs bedroom.

No answer.

DING-DONG, DING-DONG. The delivery boy with red, corkscrew hair pushed impatiently on the doorbell.

"Aaron?" Addy called.

No answer all over again.

Addy pushed aside the stack of index cards she used for studying. *Lazy little brother, won't even get the door*, she thought.

KNOCK-KNOCK-KNOCK! A fist rapped on the door. "I got a pepperoni pizza out here!" a male voice called.

Addy opened the front door. She recognized the delivery boy, it was Freddy Prosser. She'd seen him earlier that day in the video store. Who could forget that ridiculous red mop on top of his head?

Freddy scratched his nose at the sight of Addy. Pretty girls made him itchy. He bent awkwardly to claw the back of his knee, balancing the pizza box with one hand. "Addy Wheeler. Twice in one day, lucky me," he finally said.

Addy smiled, waiting.

Freddy gestured with the pizza box. "That

will be sixteen dollars and ninety-five cents—plus tip," he added with a grin.

"Hold on a sec," Addy said. "I think my mom left a twenty in the kitchen."

A gust of wind blew through the open door. "Come on inside, Freddy. It's starting to snow pretty hard, huh? You must be freezing." Addy took the pie and padded down the hall and into the kitchen. Freddy stood in the entranceway, arms dangling at his sides.

"Hey, Aaron? AARON!?" she called from a distant room. Addy realized that her brother might be wearing his headset. That explained the silence.

Freddy bounced on his feet, grateful to be indoors. He tried to whistle, but he had no talent for it. His lips only made an unmusical hissing sound, like a leaky balloon.

When Addy screamed—"Freddy, come quick!"—Freddy came quick.

THE BOY WHO
WASN'T THERE

The boy on the couch did not move.

He sat frozen, a game controller clutched in one hand.

"Aaron? Aaron, can you hear me?" Addy bent close to his face. She turned to Freddy, panic in her eyes. "He doesn't answer!"

At first, Freddy thought it was a trick. Like he was getting punked or something. But the boy didn't look right. His eyes were rolled up, showing mostly white. He did not blink. He did not stir. His lips were parted and his mouth was frozen into an awful frown. Only his bottom row of teeth showed through. Bizarrely, there was a dusting of snow on the boy's shoulders.

"Let's make sure he's breathing," Freddy said.

"What?"

It took a moment for Freddy's question to register. Addy placed an ear on Aaron's chest. "I can't—I don't know!" she stammered.

"Stay calm," Freddy advised.

"AARON!" she screamed.

Freddy placed a hand on Addy's shoulder. She looked like she was about to lose it. "Go into the kitchen and fill a glass of water, Addy. Then drink the whole thing. Then get me a hand mirror or something," he said.

A television screen flickered in the

opposite corner of the room. Freddy glanced at it. Some guy surrounded by wolves. Pretty cool.

Addy returned with the mirror. Freddy held it to Aaron's mouth. The mirror clouded up, faded, clouded again. The boy was breathing, faintly. "He's okay," Freddy said. Addy touched her brother's face, his forehead, his hands. "He's so cold," she said. She brushed the snow off his shoulders. "Snow? I don't understand."

"Maybe he stepped out," Freddy ventured. "Hit his head or something?"

Addy frowned. "There's no blood, no wound. This doesn't make sense."

"We've got to call nine-one-one," Freddy said. "You have your cell? I left mine in the car."

Addy wasn't listening. She kept tugging at her little brother, calling his name. She grabbed the microphone to his headset, "Aaron, Aaron, Aaron?"

Freddy glanced around the room, hoping to locate a phone. The television screen caught his eye again. It was snowing. A figure in some kind of hooded robe frantically waved a torch before a pack of wolves.

"Aaron!" Addy pleaded in a louder voice. She ripped the headset off his ears. "Can you hear me? Do something. Blink, move a finger, show me that you know I'm here!"

The figure on the television screen paused for a moment. He tilted his head, as if listening to a sound off in the far distance. Then he pulled down his hood and looked directly out from the television.

It appeared as if he was gazing directly into the living room.

"Look, Addy," Freddy said. He squeezed her arm. "Look!"

"What? I—"

Addy shifted her body around to see the television set. "That's him," she gasped. "That's my brother. That's . . . Aaron."

The boy inside the video game nodded once and turned away again to face the wolves.

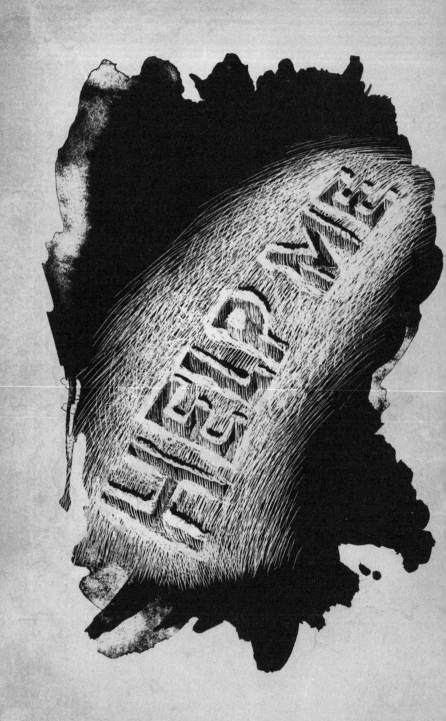

A GREAT LEAP

Aaron inspected the torch. It was burning down, dropping gray ash. The flame wouldn't last much longer. The wolves were patient. They sat on their haunches, biding time. The biggest wolf—the black one with the scar—lay down in the snow. After it lay down, the others in the pack followed suit.

The wolves were willing to wait for their next meal.

Aaron was surrounded on all sides. Behind him loomed the great, iron fence.

He was trapped.

The flame began to sputter, like a candle in the wind.

Again he felt it, *a presence*.

Someone was watching him. He felt like a character in a movie. And he sensed something else: Whoever was watching Aaron, he or she was rooting for him.

He was not alone after all.

It gave him an idea. Acting quickly, Aaron dragged a heel across the snow. Up, across, down. Up, across, across, across . . .

Back in the living room, Addy continued to stare at the television. "What's he doing?" Addy asked.

"He's making letters in the snow," Freddy said. "See that? "H—E—"

"It's a message. '*Help me*,'" Addy read.

"Is he talking to us?" Freddy asked. He looked at Aaron's frozen body on the couch. The game controller was still in his hands. "I'm telling you, Addy. This is seriously weird."

"He needs our help," Addy pleaded. "Or those wolves—"

She could not finish the sentence.

Freddy again eyed the game controller. Aaron's fingers were wrapped loosely around it. With a gentle tug, Freddy removed it from Aaron's grasp.

"What are you doing?" Addy asked.

"I'm a gamer," Freddy said. "Maybe that's the help he needs."

He studied the controls, testing the analog stick. Nothing he touched seemed to have any effect on Aaron.

"The wolves are moving closer," Addy said. "Do something!"

"Quiet, I'm trying to think!" Freddy snapped. He looked up at Addy. Tears pooled in her eyes. "I'm sorry, Addy," he said. "But you can't freak out right now. It's not okay. You have to stay strong."

Addy nodded sharply. "Okay, you're right. I can do this."

He focused his efforts on the colored buttons, yellow, red, green, blue. He tried them individually, then together, in pairs: yellow-red, red-green, and so on. Nothing worked. In frustration, Freddy prodded both analog sticks forward, placed his palm so that it covered all four buttons . . .

. . . and pushed hard.

A tremendous surge of energy, like an electrical current, raced through Aaron's body.

He felt powerful.

Aaron hurled the dying torch into the midst of the wolf pack. They scattered in panic. Aaron turned and took long, powerful strides toward the fence. He pushed off his right foot and soared up and up, leaping over the fence in a giant bound.

He landed on both feet, **OOOMPH**, tumbled forward, rolled once, and stood—stunned and amazed at the impossible thing he had just done.

How did I do that? he wondered.

SNOW GUARDS OF THE CASTLE

Holy wow," Freddy said.

"You did it!" Addy squealed. "How did he jump like that? What did you do, Freddy?"

"I just pushed a lot of buttons," he said. "It must have activated some kind of 'enhance' function."

He could see that Addy didn't understand. She wasn't a gamer.

He said, "When a character is enhanced,

a gamer makes that character run faster or jump higher for a brief burst of time."

"But you are talking as if my brother—Aaron Wheeler—is a character in a video game."

Freddy's eyes shifted from the television set, back to Addy. He didn't say a word. He just sat on the couch, next to the frozen body of a boy.

A boy who was not there.

It could not be real. It was impossible. But here they were. Freddy waited for Addy's mind to accept the impossible thing.

Finally, Addy seemed to snap awake from a trance. She stared at the television screen. "We've got to find a way to bring him home."

"I think the castle is our best hope," Freddy said. He pressed buttons, toggled forward, and hoped that Aaron received the message.

"What are you trying to do?" Addy asked.

Freddy stared up at her for a moment. Man, her eyes were blue and round and looked right at him. Drop-dead gorgeous. He never in a million years imagined he'd be alone with Addy Wheeler. The guys would never believe this. He told her, "I'm a gamer, and when you play, there's only one way out. To save your brother, we're going to have to beat the game."

The wolves snarled from the other side of the fence.

Aaron was safe.

A new feeling prodded at him, though, like he was being poked. Now he felt powerfully drawn—almost pulled by a magnet—to reach the safety of the gray castle. Okay, no problem. The castle wasn't far, just up the hill. He began to walk.

As he drew closer, Aaron smiled at the sight of a half dozen snowmen of various shapes and sizes scattered on the hill. It was as if a group of schoolchildren had built them during recess, but had to run inside before the job was finished. The snowmen wore hats and scarves, with carrot noses and broken sticks for arms.

A chill shuddered through Aaron. He stopped in his tracks. A memory flashed in his mind, a fragment of a dream from his childhood.

He had been a little boy, maybe 3 or 4, and had just seen *Frosty the Snowman* for the first time. The video scared him for some crazy reason, the way little kids are scared by ordinary things. That night, Aaron was chased in his dreams by an evil creature and he woke up screaming.

"Mom, Dad!" he cried.

His parents rushed into his bedroom and held Aaron tight. "It was just a bad dream," his mother said, over and over. "Just a bad dream."

Aaron's heart hammered in his chest.

He remembered the dream.

And he remembered the creature that had chased him in his dream.

Aaron looked up at the army of snowmen waiting at the top of the hill. Yes, he had seen them all before . . . in his nightmares.

He pulled the hood low over his head, and trudged up the hill.

THE ATTACK

Climbing the hill, Aaron had a chance to get his thoughts together. He felt drawn to the castle. Something told him that's where he *needed* to go . . . if he ever wanted to get home again.

And he knew this from the bottom of his heart to the tops of his shoes: Aaron missed his family, even if it was broken.

Families, like bones, mend. Whatever happened between his mother and his father,

Aaron loved them both. He just wanted to get home.

And was willing to do whatever it took.

The castle was not very big. He saw no life on the parapet, no guards on the protective wall at the top. One yellow light flickered in the turret window. There appeared to be only one way inside: a huge, wooden door that could accommodate a car.

Strange. Did those snowmen move?

Couldn't have.

Drawing close, Aaron got a better look at the snowmen. The eyes were made of black coal. The noses were bent carrots, some outrageously long, while other noses were short and stubby. Some snowmen had mouths shaped from pebbles or broken sticks. Eeriest of all, one had no mouth at all.

Aaron's heart hit PAUSE. He was certain that one of those snowmen moved. Aaron watched from the corner of one eye as the farthest snowman's head slowly, slowly swiveled to look in Aaron's direction.

SMACK!

A snowball blasted against Aaron's chest.

WHACK!

The thin, sharp stick of an arm whipped across his legs.

It was the snowmen, they were attacking him like fierce soldiers defending the castle. The snowmen—or guards, or whatever they were—moved steadily forward. The nearest one slashed at Aaron with its long, stick arms. Aaron's face got cut. Drops of blood splattered into the white snow. Aaron's blood. He ducked and dove out of the way. All the while, a steady bombardment of snowballs battered his body. An iceball smashed against the side of Aaron's head. He saw the stars of the night sky as he collapsed to the ground.

The snow guards of the old gray castle gathered close around Aaron's fallen body. In a haze, Aaron fought to ignore the searing pain. He lifted his head. The snow guards observed him through their cold, blank eyes. Another stick came down on Aaron's head.

CRACK!

He was out cold.

Aaron didn't feel a thing when the snow guards lifted him up high over their heads and carried him into the castle.

He just slept, a dull and dreamless sleep.

For there were no dreams in **NIGHTMARELAND**.

CRACK

NO WORRIES

In the Wheeler living room, the television set went black. No picture.

Freddy slammed down the controller in frustration. "It's not working!" he screamed. "I can't do it. I thought I had him there for a while—like I was helping him, you know—but then he got hit in the head by that hunk of ice. It went blank after that."

He ran both hands through his wild hair. "I can't do it," he repeated.

Addy spoke in a soft, firm voice. "You can do it, Freddy. You'll figure it out. I bet you've beaten plenty of games before."

Freddy looked up. He nodded, sure, but those were *games*.

"It's not easy, right?"

"No, it's mad hard," Freddy replied.

"But you never give up, Freddy. That's the thing. You keep trying." She urgently squeezed his arm. "Freddy, I need you to save my brother."

Addy's cell phone buzzed. She looked at the number and went pale. She told Freddy, "It's my mother."

He shook his head. "She'll think you're nuts," he warned.

Addy answered the phone in a too-cheerful voice. "Mom! Hi! How's it going?"

"Just checking in," Mrs. Wheeler said.

Addy told her mother that everything

was fine. Mrs. Wheeler said the roads were getting dangerous. She was thinking about getting a room in the hotel, waiting out the storm. "Would you kids be all right?" she asked.

Addy looked at her brother frozen on the couch. She saw that a cut had formed across his face. He was bleeding. A dark bruise appeared on the side of his other cheek.

"We're fine, Mom. No worries. We're great. Everything's . . . just peachy."

PRISONER IN THE TURRET

When Aaron awoke, his mind was in a fog. He felt groggy, like Rip Van Winkle emerging from a twenty-year nap. He felt a throbbing in his head.

BOOM, BOOM, BOOM.

He was sprawled on a stone floor. The air was cold and the room was dark.

"Hello?" he croaked.

His throat felt dry, his lips chapped. He wished for water.

The word echoed off the walls.

HELLO,
HELLOOO,
HELLOOOOo . . .

There was no answer.

Aaron leaned on an elbow, and pushed himself into a seated position. He had a dream-like memory of being carried up the winding, spiral steps of the castle. Then a door opened and he was tossed inside this room. The door closed, and blackness finally covered all.

Aaron was alone. This was the worst nightmare of all. Alone in the dark, far from the people who loved him.

His head slowly cleared. The room had one high window in the shape of a keyhole.

Outside it, a quarter moon shined. It was the only source of light.

His thoughts turned to his family: Addy, Grams, his mother, and his father. He wanted to get back to them more than anything in this world. He thought of the game. Somehow Aaron had become a character trapped inside **NIGHTMARELAND**. It was confusing. All Aaron knew for sure was that he was *not* where he was supposed to be.

This was not his world, not where he belonged.

After a brief inspection of his surroundings, Aaron learned that the room was perfectly round. It had no furniture, nothing at all, except for one thin blanket. *I'm inside the turret*, Aaron concluded.

He found the door and pulled. It was locked. He was a prisoner of the castle. The keyhole-shaped window beckoned to him.

He needed to climb up there somehow, get a better look, figure out a way back home.

But how?

~m~

The television screen was still blank. Freddy rubbed his eyes. His shoulders sagged, exhausted. "I'm stuck," he groaned. "It's like I've hit a wall."

"Maybe I should try," Addy offered.

Freddy shrugged.

Addy picked up the controller. She randomly pushed a series of buttons.

"What are you doing?" Freddy asked.

"I have no idea!" Addy snapped. **WHAM!** She slammed the controller on the table. The picture on the television seemed to shiver. Addy looked closer. It wasn't blank—it was just very dark. She

found the remote and adjusted the bright-
ness. Now she recognized a faint shadow
pacing back and forth.

Freddy leaned forward. "You did something when you slammed it on the table,
Addy. Put on the headset," he urged.

"No, I don't know anything—you're the
expert," Addy protested.

"I've tried everything," Freddy said.
"You're his sister. You guys have a special
connection, brother and sister. Maybe he'll be
able to hear *you*."

Addy picked up the headset.

"Aaron," she whispered into the microphone.

A chill ran down Aaron's spine.

He stood, listening.

Because he had heard his name spoken in a
whisper across a heartbreaking distance.

"Aaron," the voice said again. "I'm here."

Aaron was certain that it was Addy. She was calling to him. Sending him strength.

Freddy reached over, placed the edge of his hand on all four colored buttons. He told Addy to push both analog sticks forward. "Now," he said, and pressed down with his hand.

Aaron moved quickly beneath the high window. He squatted down—his thigh muscles felt incredibly strong—and up he rose in a tremendous jump. Aaron's fingers gripped the edge of the sill. He hung there for a moment, his strength failing, but then another surge of power whispered through his body.

He hoisted himself up to the window's narrow ledge.

Aaron's hopes fell when he looked out at the surrounding landscape. He must have been fifty feet in the air. There was no way down. No ladders, no stairs, no rope, no trees.

A crazy thought wormed its way into his mind.

It was weird, because it was a thought that Aaron knew he didn't think. Not by himself. It wasn't *his* idea, it was an idea that was *given* to him.

"*Climb down, Aaron. Push open the window. Climb like a spider. It's the only way. You can do it, little brother. Climb.*"

THE FINAL TASK

Aaron hesitated.

If he were to fall . . .

Well, he could not fall.

Failure was not an option.

The castle walls were made of rough stone. Not smooth, but jagged. With nooks and crevices, small holes and bumps.

Maybe he could climb down after all.

The first step was the hardest, because it took the most courage. Aaron lowered himself outside the window. His right foot found a thin ledge. He moved his left hand along the wall until it came to a depression in the rock.

Every movement was guided by instinct. Aaron's chest scraped against the stone. His hands pawed the wall, blindly searching for any crevice. His muscles burned, his fingers grew numb. And still, Aaron climbed down. His feet felt along the wall, seeking any foothold, no matter how small. His legs trembled from the strain. Aaron fought with everything he had. He endured every ache and pain. All the while, he felt a great strength in his body. He sensed his sister's faith. *"You can do it, Aaron. I believe in you."* And in that way, inch by inch, Aaron made his way toward the ground.

Suddenly a snowball exploded above his head, sending ice down the back of his neck. Then another, and another. He got hit in the legs and in the back. Aaron craned his neck around. The guards assembled below, firing snowballs, iceballs, and rocks with deadly accuracy.

There was no choice. If he got hit in the head now, it would be all over.

Aaron pushed himself away from the wall and back-flipped through the air. He landed on top of the nearest snowman, demolishing it. **WHOOMPH, UNGGHH.** A stick arm sliced down and missed Aaron by inches. He rolled away and sprang to his feet.

―――――――

In the living room, Addy and Freddy stood, staring at the screen.

"He made it!" Addy cheered. "They can't catch him now."

A message scrolled across the television:

FINAL GAME TASK:
DEFEAT THE LEADER AND THE GAME PLAYER
EARNS HIS FREEDOM.

"What's that mean?" Addy asked.

"If we want to defeat the game, your brother has to destroy the biggest snow creature," Freddy said.

Addy still had the controller in her hands. Freddy urged her on. "Think hard, Addy. Send him your thoughts. Somehow you've got to let Aaron know what he must do."

In a firm, clear voice, Addy whispered into the microphone . . .

In that instant, Aaron knew what he must do.

The largest, thickest, most-frightening snow creature heaved forward. There was something in its blank eyes that terrified

Aaron. Something . . . not human. Not even animal. This was a monster without a heart, without feelings. It moved toward Aaron without cruelty or kindness. It simply had one simple mission: *to kill*.

Aaron could still run. He was fast. He could run and not be caught. But that was not his choice.

Aaron had to stand and fight.

It was the only way home.

The creature's stick arms whipped furiously at Aaron, who ducked out of the way. He rolled and tumbled, darted and retreated. The monster moved steadily forward. **WHACK, WHACK, WHACK,** its arms windmilled through the air, slashing with deadly menace.

Aaron studied the pattern of the attack. He waited, and counted the seconds between each vicious blow. Suddenly Aaron reversed direction and charged forward, slamming his body hard into the snowman. **THUD**, it hurt.

The cold, black eyes of the snow creature gazed down at the small boy.

The monster raised its right arm to deliver the final blow.

A WINDOW BETWEEN TWO WORLDS

Aaron spun around. With both hands, he grabbed the creature's left arm and yanked it completely out of its body. Now Aaron twirled again, wielding the stick above his head like a sword.

In one smooth, slashing motion, with one devastating stroke—*WHOOOOSH!*—he separated the head from the snow creature's body. It fell to the ground and rolled to Aaron's feet.

Its mouth opened one final time.

It formed the shape of a silent scream.

Aaron blinked, panting. A tremor suddenly shook his body and **WHISK**, he was gone.

Or he was back again.

Home.

Inside his real body.

He shivered.

"Look, Addy. He's back!" Freddy said.

Aaron blinked. He stiffly brought a hand up to rub the back of his neck. He felt cold, so cold. He felt the trickle of blood on his face. "Hey," he said to Addy in a soft, dry whisper.

Addy didn't say a word.

She just hugged him, tight, for a very long time.

"How did I get back?" he asked.

"You beat the game," Freddy said. "When you knocked the head off that snow *thingy*, whatever it was, it opened a portal that allowed you to travel back."

"A portal?" Addy asked.

"A window, an opening between the two worlds," Freddy said.

"Whatever," Addy smiled. "I'm just glad Aaron's back."

She gave Freddy a kiss. "Thank you, Freddy. You're the best."

Freddy's face turned red. He was unable to speak.

AH-OOOOOOO! the wind howled outside. **OWWWWWWWWL!**

Aaron rose uneasily. His bones felt stiff. He shivered again, as warmth began to enter his body.

OWWWWWWWWWL!

The wind?

Aaron looked at the trees outside the

window. The branches were still. There was no wind.

AH-OOOOOOO! the howl came again.

He knew the creatures that made that sound.

"Wolves," Aaron said.

THWACK!

A snowball smashed against the living room window. Then another, and another rattled the panes.

CRASH! A window shattered, sending shards of glass everywhere.

"What's happening?" Addy screamed.

Aaron looked out on the back lawn as an army of snowmen gathered there. A pack of ugly, hungry wolves sniffed the grounds. The big black one, with a scar that zigzagged across its face, howled at the moon.

"The portal!" Aaron exclaimed. "They followed me through the portal!"

BOOM, BOOM, BOOM! The front door thundered. A headless snow creature threw its massive bulk against the door, again and again. The hinges strained from the force of the blows.

Addy frantically looked around for a weapon, a brick, a bat, *anything* she could use in the fight. Finding nothing, Addy grabbed a thick, hardcover book off the shelf.

Freddy grinned at her, cool even in a moment of panic. "What are you gonna do with that, Addy? Read to them? We can't stay and fight. We have to get out of here. NOW!"

Aaron glanced at the television set. The **NIGHTMARELAND** disk was still inside his game console.

The front door buckled. It wouldn't last much longer.

"They've nearly broken through!" Freddy warned. "Do you have a basement?"

"No, we're safe here," Aaron said. "Enough's enough."

He moved to the television set, bent down, and pulled the plug from the wall socket.

The television powered off.

In that instant, the wolves vanished and the snow guards disappeared.

The nightmare was over.

Addy, Freddy, and Aaron stood together amidst the shattered glass and broken window. Stunned and shaken. It took a long time for the terror to leak out from their bodies.

"Well," Freddy broke the silence. He rubbed his belly. "Anybody want a slice of pizza?"

Addy's cell phone buzzed. She listened for a few moments, nodding. She replied, "Sure, Mom. I know you didn't get a chance to talk to him before. No, there's nothing to worry about. He's right here."

She handed the phone to Aaron.

"Hey, Mom. Yeah, everything's great. We'll see you tomorrow, right?" Aaron listened, then smiled. "Of course, Mom. I understand. You don't think I should play video games all night long. I know, I know. Too much screen time rots my brain cells. No worries, I think I'm done with video games for today. I'll read a book instead.

"Oh, and Mom? I was using the Wii before—playing tennis—and the controller slipped out of my hand. I'm thinking we might need a new window."

SO, THE STORY ENDS. THE BOOK NEARS ITS FINAL PAGE. PERHAPS SOON, YOU'LL DISCOVER AN OLD VIDEO GAME THAT'S BEEN FORGOTTEN. GO AHEAD, DUST IT OFF, AND SLIP THE DISK INTO THE GAME CONSOLE. WHAT COULD POSSIBLY GO WRONG?

A LITTLE SCREEN TIME NEVER HURT ANYONE.

BUT FIRST, A LITTLE FRIENDLY ADVICE: YOU MIGHT WNAT TO UN-PLUG BEFORE IT'S TOO LATE . . . OR YOU MIGHT BECOME TRAPPED IN THE DARK CORNERS OF YOUR IMAGINATION WITH NO WAY TO ESCAPE.

LOOKING FOR MORE
THRILLS AND CHILLS?

DON'T MISS THE FIFTH

SCARY TALES

BOOK . . .

JAMES PRELLER

ONE-EYED DOLL

SCARY ~~TALES~~

Illustrated by IACOPO BRUNO

PERHAPS ONE DAY YOU FIND A SMALL
BOX, JUST LIKE THE KIDS IN THIS
STORY. MAYBE YOU AND YOUR FRIENDS
WILL DIG IT UP. THERE MIGHT BE
A PADLOCK ON IT. AND YOU'LL
WONDER . . .

"WHAT'S INSIDE?"

IS IT SOMETHING WONDERFUL?
TREASURE? RICHES? FORTUNE?

MAYBE, JUST MAYBE, THERE'S
SOMETHING IN THE BOX THAT SHOULD
NEVER GET OUT. NO, IT SHOULD
STAY BURIED FOREVER. LOCKED AWAY.
IMPRISONED. GONE, FORGOTTEN.

THAT'S OUR FREE ADVICE FOR THE
DAY, DEAR READER. DON'T YOU DARE
OPEN THAT BOX.

MALIK AND TIANA

The Rice children, Malik and Tiana, often played Treasure Hunt together—especially during the oven-hot days of summer. They had never discovered any actual treasure, but that didn't stop them from trying. Some days they found golf balls, weird rocks, old bottles. Mostly the hunt was just an excuse to wander under the cool umbrella of the dark woods. It was, they agreed, a good way to kill the blistering, hot days.

Besides, you never know. As Malik said, "We're not gonna find treasure, Tiana, if we never go looking for it."

Malik was ten years old. He was "the responsible one." The serious one. Good teeth, clean hands. The boy who could be trusted to look after his little sister, wild Tiana, and keep her from harm.

Malik didn't mind. Not much, anyway. He might even tell you that he loved his sister's wild black curls, her thin muscular arms, the way she seemed to float across rooms in yellow dresses. On some days, of course, Malik would frown and darken his gaze. It was hard to always be the responsible one. Like a weight he carried on his shoulders, day after day.

"No, Tiana, get off that ledge."

"Put that down, Tiana. That's glass."

"Not now, Tiana, Daddy's sleeping. Leave him be."

Their father, Mr. Charles Rice, worked nights at the factory. Malik never figured out what exactly his daddy did there, except that he returned home bone-tired and ready for bed. Right about the time most folks were getting up! Because of that simple fact—"Papa needs his sleep"—there was much tiptoeing around the house. Mama always said things like, "Shush, children," and "Quiet now, Papa's sleeping." School days, it wasn't too bad. Off on the bus they'd go, *clackety-clack*, and away they went. But in the summer when Malik and Tiana were footloose and free, the house felt like a musty old library. Hush now, children, don't say a word. Malik figured it was best to get outdoors and greet the day.

Most mornings, Mama went off to her job (Mama worked in the kitchen at the "old age" home). Everybody in the Rice family had a job, she said, even Malik and Tiana.

Malik's job was looking after his free-spirited sister. Tiana's job? Nobody had quite figured that out. She smiled and laughed, twinkled and danced. Maybe that was her role after all, just to shine like the sun. Tiana was a happy soul, so maybe making folks happy was her task in life. She lit up rooms like a 100-watt bulb. She laughed and the world laughed with her.

One bad day, Tiana wandered over to the old place. That was the name of it, exactly that: the old place. Ask anybody in the neighborhood, they'd all know the spot you were talking about. The old, abandoned house at the edge of the woods. It was a falling-down, battered old place that had been empty for years. A real eyesore, everybody called it. One shudder swung loose on a nail—*bang, bang, bang*—and slammed against the house like a warning in the wind. Haunted, maybe.

Nobody remembered folks ever living there, or if they did recall it, they didn't say so. Except to repeat, "Now, you kids, stay away from that old place."

That was the warning heard up and down the block.

Stay away from that old place.

"Why?" the children sometimes asked.

And the answer was always the same, "Nothing good can come of it, that's all. Just stay away. Understand?"

Malik and Tiana nodded their heads.

They understood.

At least, one of them did.

The other one wasn't as good at listening.

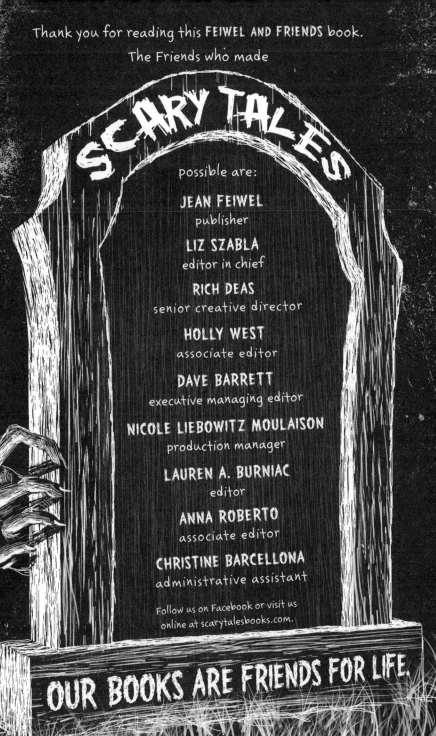

Thank you for reading this FEIWEL AND FRIENDS book.
The Friends who made

SCARY TALES

possible are:

JEAN FEIWEL
publisher

LIZ SZABLA
editor in chief

RICH DEAS
senior creative director

HOLLY WEST
associate editor

DAVE BARRETT
executive managing editor

NICOLE LIEBOWITZ MOULAISON
production manager

LAUREN A. BURNIAC
editor

ANNA ROBERTO
associate editor

CHRISTINE BARCELLONA
administrative assistant

Follow us on Facebook or visit us
online at scarytalesbooks.com.

OUR BOOKS ARE FRIENDS FOR LIFE.